Black and White

David Macaulay

WARNING

This book appears to contain a number of stories that do not necessarily occur at the same time. Then again, it may contain only one story. In any event, careful inspection of both words and pictures is recommended.

Houghton Mifflin Company

Boston

Problem Parents

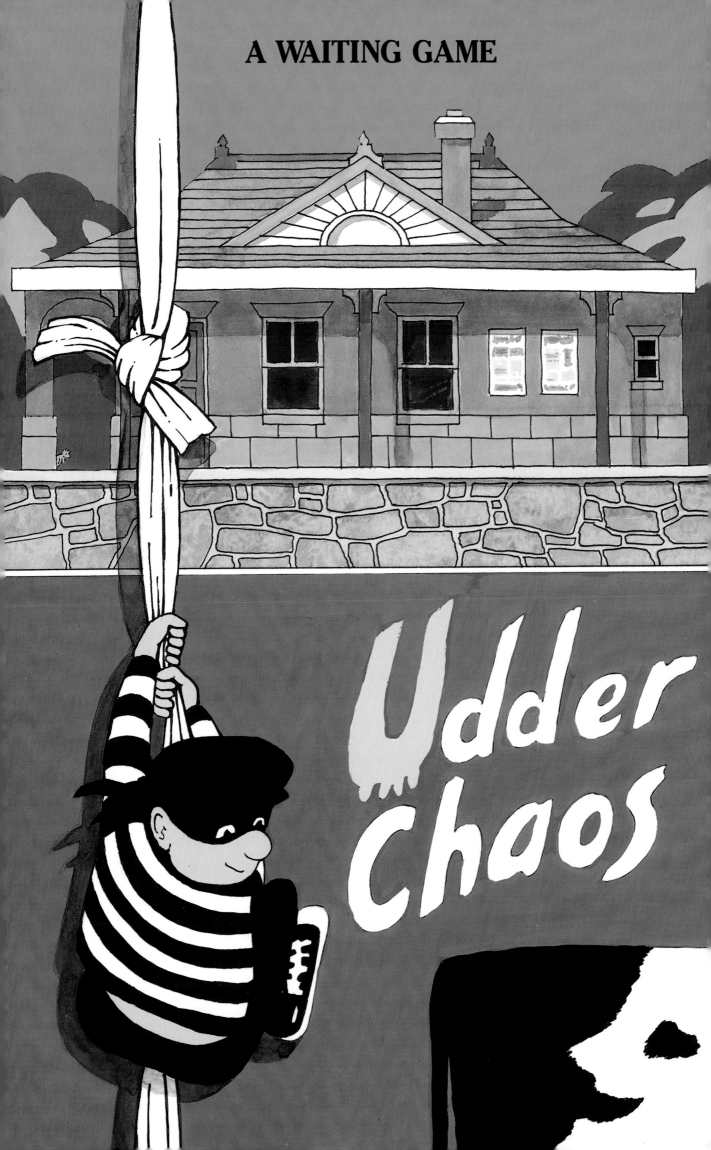

It is the boy's first trip alone. He can hardly wait to see his parents again. Even on the fast train, the journey will take all night. He sleeps curled up at one end of the seat.

One thing about parents is that you're supposed to be able to count on them, even when they don't understand you.

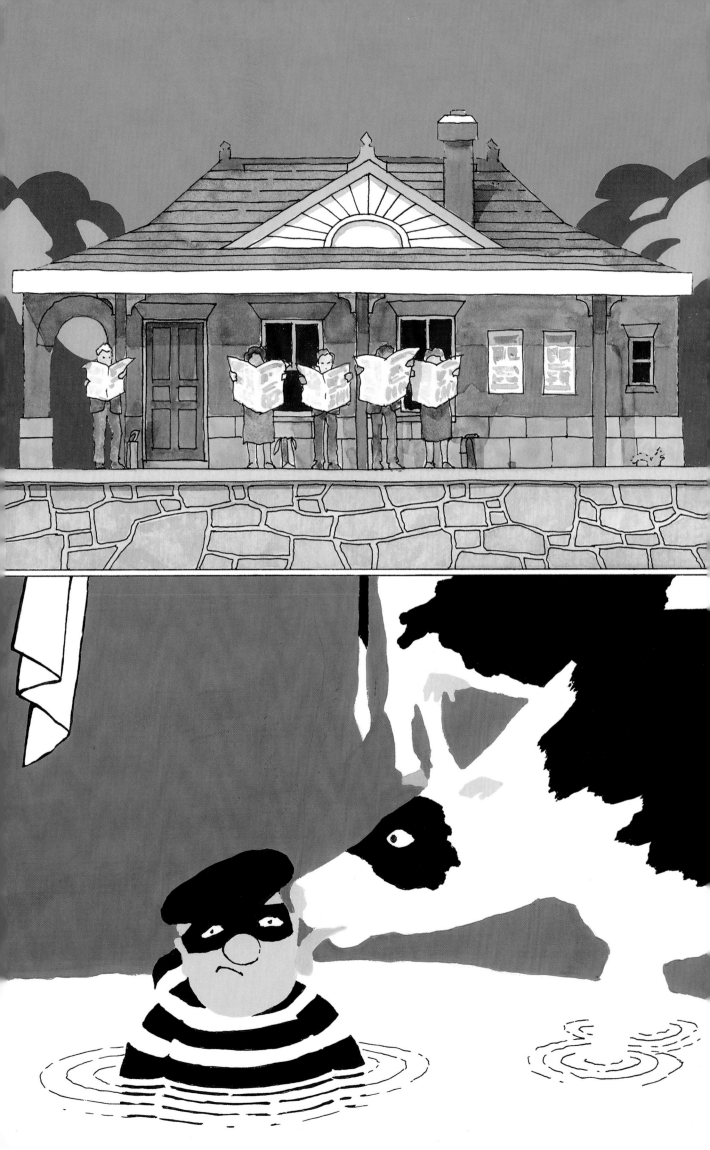

Sometime in the early morning hours, the train comes to rest. All is quiet. Suddenly, the door of the compartment slides open. The conductor leans in, announces that something is blocking the tracks, and disappears. A few minutes later, an old woman enters the compartment and sits down opposite the boy. She says nothing.

Every morning at seven o'clock they leave for their offices in the city.

The worst thing about Holstein cows is that if they ever get out of the field, they're almost impossible to find.

Leaning out the window, the boy can just make out what looks like a row of boulders in front of the train. He wonders if it's an avalanche. But where from? Even in the poor light, there is no sign of a mountain or even a hill.

And every evening at seven o'clock they come home, sort through the mail, ask about homework, and send us to bed.

Ask any farmer. It's a nightmare.
But it happens.

He sees the driver jump down from the engine and approach the boulders. The man is shouting and waving his fists. The boy grins. He's helped his parents in the garden often enough to know that you can't move rocks just by shouting at them.

But from the moment they came through the door that night, my brother and I knew something was wrong.

Your attention please. Passengers awaiting the arrival of the eight-thirteen
to the city are advised that that train will be slightly delayed.
Southern Rail regrets any inconvenience.

Amusement quickly turns to amazement. He rubs his eyes again and again but still can't believe what he sees. The boulders are moving.

That was the night they came home wearing newspapers. I couldn't believe it. They came in laughing, ignored the mail, and started marching around the living room singing, "She'll be coming 'round the mountain when she comes." I mean, you expect parents to be weird, but this was scary.

CHOIR
FESTIVAL
→

Slowly, they float off
the tracks, down the
embankment, and into
the bushes that border
the railway line.

The next thing I
knew, Dad had
lugged in a pile of
old newspapers from
the garage. He and
Mom were looking
us up and down
and whispering.

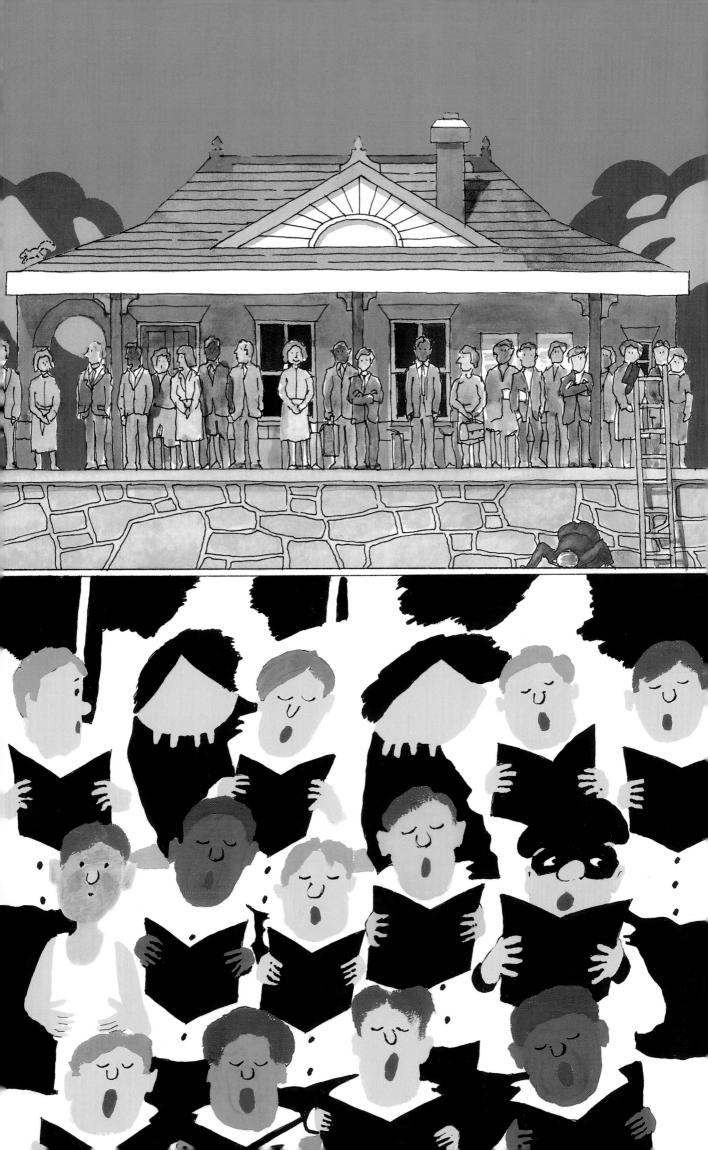

When the last one is gone, the driver clambers back into the cab and the train lurches forward. Lighter-than-air boulders tumble around the boy's mind until the steady rhythmic clicking of the rails sends him back to sleep.
Screeching brakes. Hissing steam. Singing. Singing?! Reluctantly, he opens his eyes. The old lady has vanished.

I asked if they wanted to check my homework. Mom just tore the Leisure section into strips and asked if I wanted to be a turkey!

Your attention please. Passengers awaiting the arrival of the eight-thirteen to the city are advised that that train is still temporarily delayed. Southern Rail regrets any inconvenience.

And they're no easier to find
at night...

With his sleeve, he clears some mist from inside the window. Where he expects a platform, he sees only smoke or steam or cloud. He stares and wonders. Is that really cloud out there?

I looked at my brother. We played along—for the moment. But pretty soon both of us looked like rejects from some origami zoo. I was thinking, "Who *are* these people?"

even with
a light.

And something else is
drifting by. Snow?
The boy is thrilled.
He opens the window.
The singing gets louder.

Then they started
marching again and,
by the fourth trip
around the living
room, my brother
was really getting
into it. The little
traitor.

He opens the window.
The singing gets louder.

He sticks out his hand to

catch

a few

flakes.

I knew I was the only one who could save them now! I grabbed the mail and stuffed it into my father's hand. He stopped. I held my breath. He shuffled through it. I crossed my fingers. He shuffled again and then ripped it into a million pieces and I was standing in the middle of a blizzard.

Your attention please. Passengers still awaiting the arrival of the eight-thirteen to the city are advised that Southern Rail has no idea where the train is and regrets any inconvenience.

He's about to melt them on his tongue when he notices that each flake is decorated with words and numbers. It isn't snow. It's newspaper!

I was about to give up when my brother suddenly shouted, "Let's go out for dinner."

"Good idea," said Mom. "I know just the place."

I panicked. I mean, I was still dressed like a turkey! In the house was bad enough—but outside?!

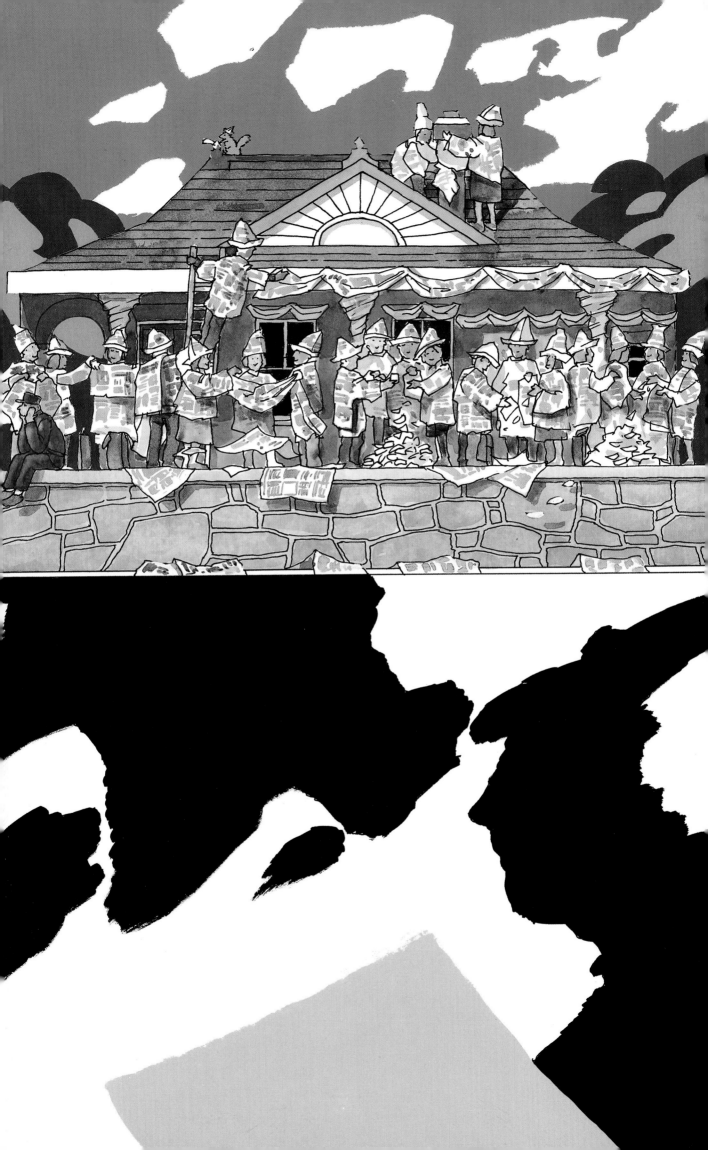

Then he sees them standing beside the train. Strange creatures tossing torn paper into the air and singing. He must have missed them at first because their clothes are as gray as the swirling cloud.

I tried one last thing. "But it's a school night! What about my homework?" (I was really desperate!) "Just give me a second to brush my hair," said Mom. Then Dad looked at me with this grin and said, "Maybe we should leave our costumes at home." I couldn't believe it. Sanity! My brother, of course, insisted on wearing his stupid hat.

Your attention please. Passengers awaiting the eight-thirteen to the city are advised that that train is now arriving on platform one. Southern Rail regrets any inconvenience caused by the delay.

A piercing whistle suddenly interrupts the celebration.

With a jolt, the train begins to move.
Quickly, the boy draws his hand inside,
letting the flakes slip away.
He yawns and settles once more
into the warmth of his seat.

In the car they started singing again. But it was pretty dark out, so I figured nobody could see us. We pulled up to the fish and chips shop. Mom went in. Soon she was back, laughing and holding our dinners—each wrapped, as usual, in newspaper. "See," she said, "everybody's doing it!"

But the best thing
about Holstein cows...

When the boy awakens, the train is drawing alongside a platform beneath an enormous glass roof. He puts his nose up against the window. No cloud. No snow. No singing. Instead, two figures approaching the train. There's something familiar about them. The boy steps onto the platform and they move quickly toward him. "Hello, my angel," his mother says. "What a journey you must have had."

I've got to admit, it was kind of fun in the end—even cleaning up all the papers around the house. But just as I was heading for bed I heard, "Hey, kiddo. What about that homework?"
You've got to watch those parents. It's exhausting.

is that no matter
how far they go,
they always come back—
when they want
to be milked.

Library of Congress Cataloging-in-Publication Data

Macaulay, David.
Black and white/David Macaulay.
    p.   cm.
Summary: Four brief "stories" about parents, trains, and cows, or
is it really all one story? The author recommends careful inspection
of words and pictures to both minimize and enhance confusion.
ISBN 0-395-52151-3
[1. Literary recreations.]   I. Title.
PZ7.M1197B1   1990   89-28888
[Fic]—dc20   CIP
                              AC

To Charlotte Valerie

7/2014